달 못

Ivan Gantschev

DER MONDSEE

Verlag Neugebauer Press, Salzburg, Austria 1981

Translated by Lᴇᴇ Mi-Rim

© Benedict Press, Waegwan, Korea 1983

달못

1983년 8월 초판 | 2007년 7월 6쇄
옮긴이 · 이미림 | 펴낸이 · 이형우

ⓒ **분도출판사**

등록 · 1962년 5월 7일 라15호
718-806 경북 칠곡군 왜관읍 왜관리 134의 1
왜관 본사 · 전화 054-970-2400 · 팩스 054-971-0179
서울 지사 · 전화 02-2266-3605 · 팩스 02-2271-3605
www.bundobook.co.kr

ISBN 89-419-8315-0 04840
값 5,000원

달 못

이야기와 그림 : 이반 간체프
옮김 : 이 미림

분도출판사

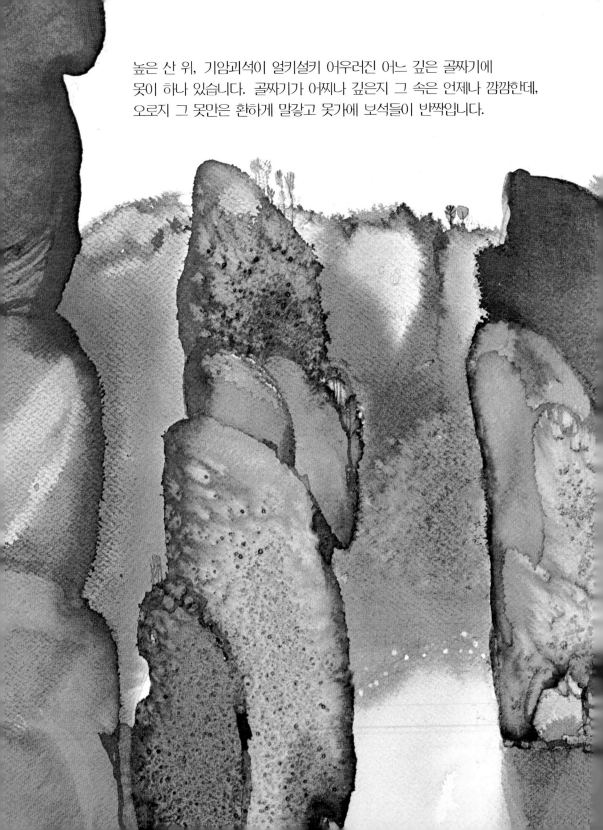

높은 산 위, 기암괴석이 얼키설키 어우러진 어느 깊은 골짜기에
못이 하나 있습니다. 골짜기가 어찌나 깊은지 그 속은 언제나 깜깜한데,
오로지 그 못만은 환하게 말갛고 못가에 보석들이 반짝입니다.

사람들이 그러는데,
이따금씩 달님이 땅을 찾아 내려오신답니다.
하늘에서 뉘엿뉘엿 얼음같이 차가운 그 못으로
멱감으러 오셨다가
부르르르르 온몸을 떨며 말리시는데,
그 바람에 그 못가에는
주르르르르 보석하고 금이랑 은 가루가 흩뿌려진다나요.

사람들은 그래서 그 못을 **달못**이라고 부릅니다.
정작 그 못이 어디 있는지 아는 사람은 아무도 없지만요.

수많은 사람들이 그 못을 찾아 보았지만 헛일이었습니다.
뽐내며 길을 나섰다가는 풀이 죽어 되돌아오기가 일쑤였지요.
더러는 영영 함흥차사가 되고 말았고요.

양치기 한 사람만 그 자리를 알았었지요.
어디 얘기를 해 줄 상대가 있어야지요?
그는 도시나 시골 마을에서 멀리 떨어진
깊은 산 속에서 양을 치며 살았습니다.
마을에서 거기까지 가려면 걸어서 꼬박
하루 낮하고 하루 밤이 걸려야 했지요.
그것도 무작정하고 빽빽한 숲을 헤치며
그루터기와 돌부리를 이리저리 넘어서요.
누가 그런 생고생을 하려 들겠어요?
그래서 그 양치기는 복돌이라는 손자하고
둘이서만 외딴 오두막집에서 살았습니다.

봄·여름·가을·겨울이 오고고 또 오고,
그럭저럭 그 양치기는 할아버지가 되고 또
점점 더 늙어 갔습니다.

겨울이면 눈이 쌓여 산길이 막혀 버렸습니다.
양치기 할아버지는 불을 쬐며 지내시고, 복돌이가 할아버지를
돌보아 드렸습니다.
"진작부터 손자 녀석에게 달못 가는 길을 가리켜 주고 싶었는데."
할아버지는 생각에 잠겼습니다.
"그 아름다운 보석들을 보여 주면 좋아할 테지."
그러나 인젠 그럴 만한 힘이 모자랐습니다.

그리고 세상을 떠나자,
그 양치기 할아버지는 비밀을 간직한 채
무덤에 묻히었습니다.

복돌이는 외톨이가 되었습니다.
혼자서 양들을 돌보았습니다.
그래도 복돌이는 만족해하며 살았습니다.
양유가 넉넉히 나므로 치즈를 만들어서
읍내에 나갈 때 내다 팔아 그 돈으로
자기하고 양들이 먹을 소금을 샀습니다.
절로 열린 능금이랑 배랑 산딸기랑을
따다가 겨울에 먹을 쨈도 고아 놓고,
양파랑 콩이랑 푸성귀는 손수 심었지요.
따끈한 국을 끓일 산나물이나 버섯도,
향기로운 약초도 곳곳이 수두룩했고요.

어느 날 저녁 양들을 우리에 몰아넣다가 보니,
한 마리가 모자랐습니다.

복돌이는 빵하고 치즈 한 토막하고 양파 몇 개를 챙겨 들고
잃은 양을 찾아 나섰습니다.
날은 벌써 저물어 가는데, 저 아래로 깊은 골짜기가 하나
아가리를 벌리고 나타났습니다. 그리고 깊숙히 밑바닥에서부터
가냘프고 속절없는 양 울음 소리가 들려 오는 것 같았습니다.
복돌이는 낭떠러지 끝까지 바짝 다가가서 아래를 엿보았습니다.
거기에는 반짝이는 못이 하나 있고, 그 못가에 벼룩처럼 쬐그맣게
잃었던 자기 양이 주인을 찾아 울부짖고 있었어요.
복돌이는 바위 틈으로 뚫린 길을 하나 찾아 내어 타고 내려갔습니다.

이윽고 밑바닥에 이르렀을 때는 마침 달이 떠오르고 있었습니다.
마치 대낮처럼 환해졌어요!
못 둘레에서는 모든 것이 반짝반짝 번쩍번쩍 빛나고 있었습니다.
온통 보석들이었어요!
복돌이는 하도 좋아서 그 중 제일 크고 가장 아름다운 것들을
메고 온 양치기 자루에다 주워 담기 시작하였습니다.

"이걸 읍내에 갖다 팔면 새 담요랑 옷 한 벌하고 소금도 듬뿍 살 수
있겠지. 또 혹시 양들이 그리 쉽사리 길을 잃지 않도록
방울종을 하나씩 달아 줄 수 있을지도 몰라."
이렇게 복돌이가 속생각을 큰 소리로 중얼거리고 있는데 난데없이
대답이 들려 왔어요.
"그럼, 네가 여기서 살아서 다시 밖으로 나갈 줄을 안다면야 그렇고말고."
복돌이가 흘깃 뒤돌아보니, 멋지되 큼직한
은빛 여우 한 마리가 있었어요. 여우는
먹을 것이 있으면 좀 주겠느냐고 물었습니다. 그리고
"그러면 큰 비결을 하나 가르쳐 주지."
하고 보답을 약속했습니다.
"내가 가진 것은 얼마든지 줄게."
소년이 말했습니다.
"많지는 않아. 빵 조금하고 치즈하고 양파 몇 개야."
여우는 깡그리 게걸스레 먹어 치우더니,
충고를 해 주었습니다. 해가 뜨기 전에 못을 떠나라고요.
"해가 뜨면 보석에 눈이 부시어 멀어.
그래서 영영 집으로 돌아가지 못하게 돼.
따라와, 올라가는 길을 가리켜 줄게."

복돌이는 양을 어깨에 둘러 메었습니다.
여우 덕분에 골짜기를 곧 빠져 나와서
새로 친구가 된 여우와 작별한 다음,
복돌이는 양을 데리고 해가 뜨기 전에
무사히 오두막집으로 돌아왔어요.

며칠 후, 복돌이는 읍내로 나갔습니다.
거기 장터에서 헝겊에 보석을 차려 놓고
전을 벌였는데 ― 아이고!
어느새 임금님의 병사들이 와서 다짜고짜
따라오라고 명령하는 것이었어요.
병사들은 복돌이를 임금님의 성 안으로
데리고 갔습니다.

임금님은 그처럼 값진 보석이 어디서 났느냐고 물었고, 복돌이는
자초지종을 이실직고하였습니다. 그러자 그 보석들은 압수되고 말았고,
복돌이는 그저 처분만 기다릴 수밖에 없었습니다.
그때 임금님은 그 신비로운 못이 어디 있느냐고 물었는데,
그걸 설명하기가 어려워 복돌이는 그만 더듬거리기 시작했어요.
그러자 임금님은 노발대발하시며 바른 대로 대지 않으면
깊은 우물 속에 처넣어 버리리라고 윽박질렀습니다.

그래서 엉겁결에 복돌이는 제안하였습니다.
그 못까지 길을 안내해 드리겠다고요.
임금님은 친히 행차하시기로 하고
고문관도 두 사람 따르게 하여
모두들 함께 길을 나섰습니다.
임금님과 두 신하는 말을 타고
한밤중에 복돌이가 가리키는 대로
산길을 톺아 달렸습니다. 이따금
복돌이도 함께 태워 주었어요.
워낙 마음이 바빴거든요.
하루 밤과 하루 낮이 꼬박
걸려서 일행은 그 골짜기에
다다랐습니다.

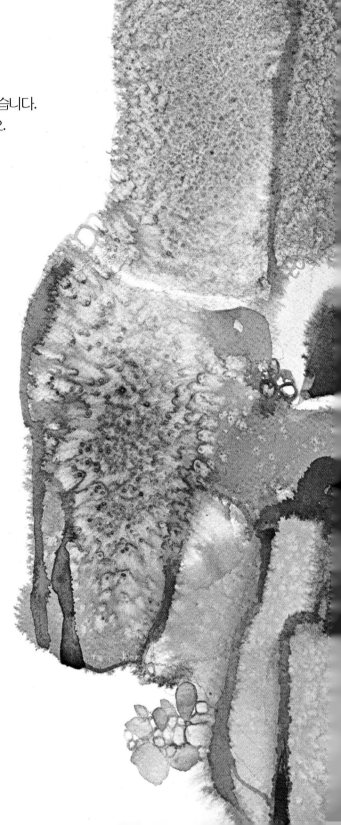

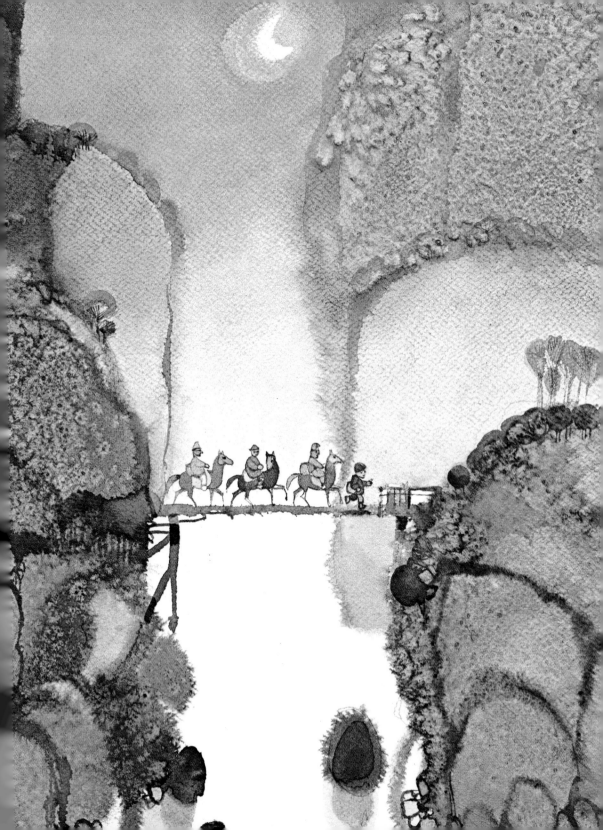

다시 달이 떠오르고 못가가 휘황찬란하게 번쩍이자 사람들은 욕심을 부리며
보석을 모았습니다. 복돌이 자신은 아무 것도 차지하지 않고 물끄러미
모두들 야단법석하는 꼴만 바라보고 섰습니다. 그러다가 여우의 충고가
생각나서 임금님에게 다가가 아뢰었습니다. "전하, 해가 뜨기 전에 이 부근을
벗어나야 하옵니다. 안 그러면 우리 모두 눈이 멀게 되옵니다." 그러나 임금님은
버럭 화를 내며 "참견 말고 꺼져! 내가 할 일은 내가 더 잘 알아!" 하였습니다.

그래서 복돌이는 더는 아무 말도 못하고 그곳을 떠났고 임금님과 두 시종은
달못 가 밑바닥에 남았습니다. 해가 뜨자 그들은 보석 빛에 부시어 눈이
멀었습니다. 아무 것도 못 보게 된 그들은 보석이 가득 찬 자루를 지고
길을 잃어버린 채 바위 틈을 더듬으며 헤매어 다니다가 깊은 골짜기에
떨어지고 말았습니다.

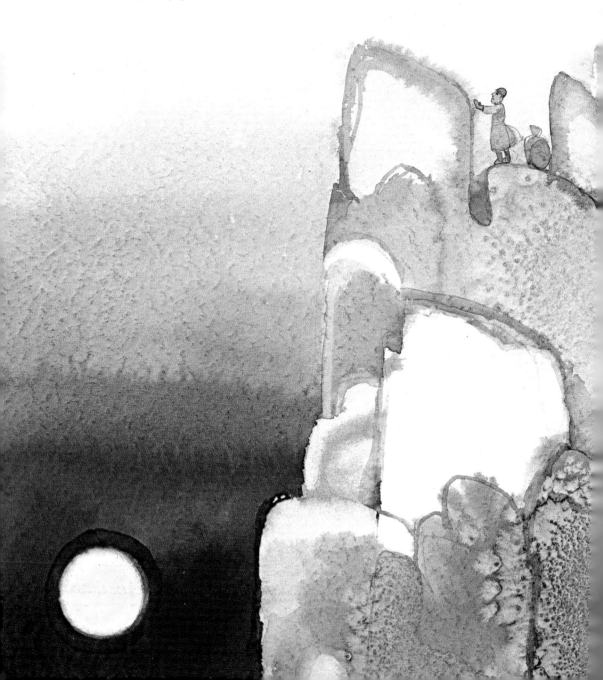

이 나으리들이 몰래 도시를 떠날 적에 낌새를 챈 사람은 아무도 없었습니다.
그래서 그들이 어디로 사라져 버렸는지 또한 아무도 몰랐습니다.
그러나 달못 가에는 다름없이 그 신비로운 광채가
일고 있었습니다.

또 한번 복돌이는 아름다운 보석을 몇 개 주워 왔습니다.
그리고 그것을 양마다 하나씩 목고리에 매달아 주었습니다.
그래서 다시는 양들이 길을 잃지 않을 수 있게 되었지요.
그 빛이 밤에도 양들이 있는 곳을 알려 주었거든요.
나머지 보석들은 창틀에다가 얹어 두었습니다.
보름달이 뜰 무렵이면 그 광채가 어찌나 밝은지
복돌이는 밤이 이슥하도록 장작을 팰 수 있었습니다.
그리고 친구 여우가 찾아올 때에는 멀리서부터 벌써
복돌이의 오두막집이 보였습니다.

DER

MONDSEE

Geschichte mit Bildern
von Ivan Gantschev,
nacherzählt von Kurt Baumann

Hoch oben in den Bergen, in einem Gewirr von Felsen und Schluchten,
liegt ein See. Die Schluchten sind so tief, daß es immer Nacht ist in ihnen.
Nur der See strahlt hell und klar.
Und seine Ufer funkeln von Edelsteinen.

Die Leute erzählen sich, daß der Mond manchmal zur Erde heruntersteige.
Auf seiner langen Bahn am Himmel ziehe es ihn zu dem eiskalten See
hinunter, um darin ein Bad zu nehmen.

Danach schüttle er sich, so daß Edelsteine,
Gold und Silberstaub nur so aufs Ufer stieben.

Deshalb nennen die Leute den See: MONDSEE. Obwohl niemand weiß,
wo er liegt.

Viele haben nach dem See gesucht, aber vergeblich.
Prahlend zogen sie aus, und kleinlaut kamen sie zurück.
Und manche kamen nie mehr zurück und blieben verschollen.

THE

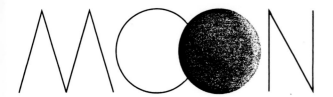

MOON LAKE

Story and pictures
by Ivan Gantschev,
translated by Oliver Gadsby

High up in the mountains, lost among rocks and ravines, there is a lake.
The ravines are so deep that the sun can't shine in them.
The rocks are old and cracked. Only the lake is bright and clear,
and its banks glisten with precious stones.

People say that sometimes the moon comes to visit the earth.
And as she comes slowly down, she always heads for the icy lake
where she likes to bathe.
After she has had her bath she shakes herself dry,
showering the banks of the lake with precious jewels, with gold-dust
and with silver.

So people call the lake Moon Lake, although no-one knows where it is
to be found.

Many people have searched for it, but always in vain.
They set out full of hope and pride, and return forlorn.
Some never do return, but are lost forever in rocky wilderness.

Nur ein Schäfer kannte den Ort.
Wem hätte er davon erzählen sollen?
Er lebte mit seinen Schafen in den Bergen, weitab von Städten und Dörfern.
Einen Tag und eine Nacht mußte man gehen, um zu ihm zu gelangen.
Durch dichte Wälder und über Stock und Stein.
Und wer wollte das schon?
So lebte er, nur mit Borka, seinem Enkelkind,
in der einsamen Hütte.

Die Jahreszeiten kamen und gingen, und der Schäfer wurde alt und älter.

Im Winter waren die Pfade verschneit.
Der alte Schäfer wärmte sich am Feuer, Borka sorgte für ihn.
„Schon lange wollte ich meinem Enkel den Weg zum Mondsee zeigen",
dachte der Alte. „Vielleicht gefallen ihm die schönen Steine."
Aber seine Kräfte reichten nicht mehr dazu aus.

Und als er starb, nahm der Alte sein Geheimnis mit ins Grab.

Borka blieb allein zurück. Allein kümmerte er sich um die Schafe.
Aber er lebte zufrieden. Milch gaben sie genug,
und er machte Käse daraus. Den verkaufte er, wenn er in die Stadt ging.
Dann kaufte er Salz für sich und die Tiere.
Von Wildäpfeln, Birnen und Himbeeren
kochte er Marmelade für den Winter.
Zwiebeln, Knoblauch und Salat pflanzte er selbst.
Brennesseln und Pilze für eine warme Suppe
fanden sich überall. Und würzige Kräuter gab es haufenweise.

Eines Abends, als er die Schafe in den Stall brachte,
merkte er, daß eines fehlte.

Borka nahm Brot, ein Stück Käse und ein Bund Zwiebeln,
dann machte er sich auf die Suche nach dem Schaf.

Only one person knew the lake: a quiet old shepherd.
Who could he have told about it?
He lived in the mountains with his sheep, far from any towns or villages.
It took a day and a night travelling to reach his cottage –
through thick forests, over hills, and down deep valleys.
And who would go through all that trouble?
So he lived in his lonely cottage, with no-one but Peter, his grandson,
to keep him company.

The years came and went and the shepherd grew older and older.

In winter, the paths were blocked by snow.
The old shepherd stayed inside keeping warm by the fire
and Peter looked after him.
"I've always wanted to show my grandson the Moon Lake,"
thought the old man. "He might like those beautiful stones."
But he wasn't strong enough to take the boy into the mountains.
When the old man died, Peter buried him close to the cottage.
And so the shepherd took his secret with him to the grave.

Peter stayed in the cottage on his own and looked after the sheep.
But he was happy. The sheep gave plenty of milk
and he used some of it to make cheese
which he could sell when he went to town.
He didn't make the journey very often, but when he did,
he bought salt for himself and the animals.
He used wild apples, pears and raspberries to make jam for the winter.
And in the garden he planted onions, beans and lettuces.

One evening, when he was driving the sheep into their stall,
he noticed that one of them was missing.

Peter took some bread, a piece of cheese and a few onions,
and set out to look for the sheep.

Es dämmerte schon, als sich unter ihm eine tiefe Schlucht öffnete.
Aus der Tiefe glaubte er, ein leises, hilfloses Blöken zu hören.
Er legte sich dicht an den Abgrund und spähte hinunter.
Dort lag ein glänzender See, und am Ufer, ganz klein wie ein Floh,
stand sein Schaf und rief nach ihm.
Borka fand einen Durchschlupf zwischen den Felsen und kletterte hinab.

Als er unten war, ging der Mond auf. Es wurde hell wie am Tage!
Um den See herum funkelte und glänzte alles.
Da waren lauter Edelsteine! Die gefielen ihm so gut, daß er anfing,
die größten und schönsten aufzuheben und in seine Schäfertasche
zu stopfen.

„Wenn ich die Steine in der Stadt verkaufen kann,
werde ich mir eine neue Decke, ein Hemd und viel Salz kaufen können,
und vielleicht noch ein Glöckchen für jedes Schaf,
damit sie nicht so leicht verloren gehen", dachte er laut vor sich hin.

„Ja, wenn du wüßtest, wie man hier wieder lebend hinausfindet",
bekam er zur Antwort.

Borka wandte sich um. Ein schöner großer Silberfuchs stand hinter ihm.
Der Fuchs fragte, ob er für ihn etwas zu essen hätte.
„Und ein großes Geheimnis werde ich dir verraten", versprach er dafür.

„Ich gebe dir gerne, was ich habe", meinte der Junge.
„Viel ist es nicht. Ein wenig Brot, Käse und einige Zwiebeln."
Doch der Fuchs fraß alles gierig auf.
Dann gab er Borka den Rat, den See noch vor
Sonnenaufgang zu verlassen.
„Wenn die Sonne am Himmel steht", sagte der Fuchs,
„wirst du von den Steinen geblendet
und findest den Weg nie mehr nach Hause.
Den Weg nach oben will ich dir zeigen."

It was beginning to get dark, when Peter came to a deep ravine.
He thought he could hear a faint, helpless bleating coming from the bottom.
So he lay on the cliff-edge and peered down.
Far beneath him he saw a glistening lake, and on its bank,
looking small and lost, was his sheep, bleating piteously up at him.
Peter found a passage between the rocks and climbed down.
When he reached the bottom, the moon was out, and he could see
as clearly as by day.
All around the lake, everything was shining and sparkling.
The banks were covered in jewels!
He liked them so much that he began picking up the biggest
and the most beautiful ones, and putting them in his shepherd's sack.

"If I can sell the stones in town,
I'll be able to buy a new blanket,
a shirt, and as much salt as I want,"
he said out loudly.

"You could, if you knew how to get out
of here alive," came the answer.

Peter spun round. Before him stood a large, handsome silver fox.
The fox asked him if he had anything to eat.   He was so hungry.
"I will let you into a big secret in return," the fox promised.

"That's all right. I'll give you what I've got anyway," said the boy.
"There isn't much: a bit of bread, some cheese and a few onions."
But the fox ate everything eagerly.
Then he told Peter the secret:
that he must leave the lake before sunrise.
"When the sun rises," said the fox,
"you will be blinded by the dazzling stones,
and you will never find your way home.
Come with me, and I'll show you the way to the top."

Borka lud sich das Schaf auf die Schulter.
Mit Hilfe des Fuchses war er bald aus der Schlucht heraus.
Er verabschiedete sich von seinem neuen Freund, dem Fuchs.
Und vor Sonnenaufgang fand er mit dem Schaf zurück zur Hütte.

Am anderen Tag trat Borka den Weg in die Stadt an.
Dort, auf dem Marktplatz, legte er seine Steine
auf einem Tuch aus und bot sie zum Verkauf an.
Aber o weh! Bald kamen die Soldaten des Königs
und befahlen ihm, mitzukommen.

Sie brachten ihn zum Schloß des Königs. Dieser wollte wissen,
woher Borka seine teuren Steine hätte. Der Junge erzählte seine Geschichte.
Da wurden ihm die Steine weggenommen, und Borka blieb nichts
anderes übrig, als sich zu fügen.
Dann wollte der König wissen, wo der geheimnisvolle See liege.
Aber das war schwierig zu erklären, und Borka fing zu stammeln an.
Der König drohte, ihn in den tiefsten Brunnen zu werfen,
wo nur Schlangen und Frösche hausten.

Da erbot sich Borka, die Männer zum See zu führen.
Der König nahm noch zwei seiner Ratgeber mit,
und zusammen machten sie sich auf den Weg.
Sie ritten bei Nacht und Dunkelheit
auf den Pfaden, die ihnen Borka wies.
Ab und zu durfte auch er aufsitzen, denn die Männer hatten es eilig.

Eine Nacht und ein Tag waren vergangen, als sie zur Schlucht kamen.

Wieder stieg der Mond auf, die Ufer des Sees glänzten,
und die Leute sammelten gierig die Edelsteine ein.
Borka selber nahm nichts, ungläubig schaute er dem Treiben zu.
Da erinnerte er sich an den Rat des Fuchses. „Mein König",
sagte er, „wir müssen vor Sonnenaufgang die Gegend verlassen,

Peter heaved the sheep on to his shoulder.
With the fox's help, he was soon out of the ravine,
and there he said goodbye to his new friend.
By sunrise, he was safely back at the cottage with his sheep.

A few days later, Peter made the journey into town.
He spread out his stones on a cloth
in the market-place and put them up for sale.
But then a terrible thing happened.
Two policemen came and ordered him to follow them.
They took him to the castle of an important minister.
He was with the police-chief, waiting for the young shepherd,
and they demanded to know where Peter had gotten the precious stones.
The boy told them his story, but they just laughed
and took the stones from him. Peter was powerless to stop them.
Then the minister wanted to know how to find the lake;
but it was difficult to explain.
The police-chief threatened to throw Peter down the deepest well,
full of snakes and frogs.

So Peter agreed to lead the men to the lake.
The minister took two other friends with him, and they all set off.
They rode through the darkness of the night
along the tracks which Peter showed them.
From time to time the men let him
ride with them on one of the horses, since they were in a hurry.

A night and a day had passed when they reached the ravine.

The moon rose as before, the banks of the lake glistened, and the men
eagerly started cramming the jewels into their sacks.

Then Peter remembered the fox's advice. "Excuse me sir,"
he said to the minister, "we must leave here before sunrise

sonst werden wir alle blind." Doch der König antwortete bloß zornig:
„Geh weg, ich weiß selbst besser, was ich zu tun habe!"
Da ging Borka wortlos davon und ließ den König und sein Gefolge
drunten am Mondsee zurück.

Als die Sonne aufging, wurden die Männer von den Steinen geblendet.
Sie konnten nichts mehr sehen. Mit vollen Säcken beladen, irrten sie zwischen
den Felsen umher und fielen dabei in tiefe Schluchten.

Niemand hatte etwas bemerkt, als die Herren heimlich die Stadt verließen.
So wußte auch niemand, wohin sie verschwunden waren.
Aber die Ufer des Mondsees leuchteten noch immer
in ihrem geheimnisvollen Glanz.

Noch einmal holte sich Borka ein paar schöne Steine.
Bei jedem Schaf befestigte er einen am Halsband.
So konnten die Schafe nicht mehr verloren gehen.
Das Licht verriet auch nachts, wo sie waren.
Die restlichen Steine legte Borka auf die Fensterbank.
Bei Vollmond leuchteten sie so stark, daß er ohne Kerzenschein
bis tief in die Nacht Holz schnitzen konnte.
Und wenn sein Freund, der Fuchs, ihn besuchen kam,
sah er die Hütte schon von weitem.

or we'll all be blinded." But the minister just replied angrily:
"Go away, you stupid little shepherd-boy!" and he boxed the boy's ears.
So Peter slipped away without saying another word, and left the police-chief,
and the minister and his friends by the lake, busily collecting jewels.

When the sun rose, the men were blinded by the dazzling stones.
Weighed down by their full sacks, they wandered amongst the rocks
until they fell into the deep ravines.

No-one had noticed the men secretly leaving the town in the night.
So no-one ever knew where they had disappeared to.
And the banks of the lake still gleam with their secret treasures.

Peter went back to the lake once, to fetch a few beautiful stones.
He tied some on to the collar of each of the sheep.
That way, they couldn't get lost, even at night
the light of the stones showed where they were.

He put the rest of the stones on his window-ledge.
When there was a full moon, they shone so brightly that Peter could
stay up carving wood until late in the night.
And when his friend the fox came to visit him, he could see the cottage
from miles away.